NOGUCHI
THE SAMURAI

BURT KONZAK

Illustrated by JOHNNY WALES

LESTER PUBLISHING LIMITED

CANADIAN CATALOGUING IN PUBLICATION DATA
Konzak, Burt, 1946–
Noguchi the samurai
ISBN 1-895555-54-X

I. Wales, Johnny. II. Title.
PS8571.059N6 1994   jC813'.54   C93-095159-X   PZ7.K65No 1994

Lester Publishing Limited
56 The Esplanade
Toronto, Ontario
Canada M5E 1A7

Printed and bound in Hong Kong
94 95 96 97 5 4 3 2 1

Acknowledgments

The author would like to express his sincere appreciation to Kathy Lowinger who was invaluable along the total path of development of this book.

Every effort has been made to make the illustrations in this book as historically accurate as possible. The illustrator would like to extend his thanks to the Royal Ontario Museum Libraries, Mr. Fred Kay of Toronto, and Mr. Saburo Yoritate and Dr. Yoshiya Kaneko of Tokyo for their invaluable assistance in supplying research materials for this book.

To my daughters, Sonya and Mélina,

to whom I have taught the art of *Karate-do*,

and who have taught me the value of gentleness,

I dedicate this book

— B. K.

I dedicate this book to the memory of my late father,

William Fenwick Wales, M.D. F.R.C.S.(C)

— J. W.

The bay separating Miya and Kuwana was once
part of the Great Eastern Road between Edo and
ancient Kyoto. The ferry docks teemed with merchants
and their wares, minstrels, and wandering monks. Sharp
smells of dried fish, incense, and oranges filled the air.

One day, when the ferry was about to set sail, Noguchi the Samurai stormed aboard. He pushed the other passengers aside, crunching toes and elbowing ribs as he stepped. He saw that they were frightened and this pleased him very much.

Noguchi found a place against the ferry's bulwark. He drew on his pipe, puffing fragrant smoke into the clear, blue air. As he tapped the pipe on the wooden gunwale, *plop*, the burning bowl disappeared into the rolling, green waters of the sea.

Noguchi's face turned a slow, ugly red. He stamped his feet, each heavy step like thunder, as if he could find his lost pipe in the terrified faces around him.

"Please, sir." A grimy hand reached up to Noguchi. "Do me the honor of taking my pipe." Kuzu-ya the rag dealer bowed low.

"How dare you insult me, impudent man! A rag man offering a samurai his pipe! Hah!" Noguchi drew his long sword from its scabbard. He was thoroughly enjoying himself.

All the passengers were swept into the
storm of his tantrum — all the passengers save
one. An elderly samurai, Michihara, his arm
crooked on his sword, snored beneath his straw
hat in the shade of the cabin's thatched roof.

The sight of the sleeping samurai enraged Noguchi. He swept his sword in a ferocious arc so close to Michihara that straw flew from the roof above his head. Michihara opened one eye. "You, Noguchi, are a bully. The sea rocks this ship enough without your help. Why don't you leave Kuzu-ya and the others in peace?"

"Because I am the greatest warrior in Japan. It is my pleasure to fight where and with whom I wish," Noguchi spat.

Kuzu-ya appealed to the elderly samurai. "Michihara, please, you must help us. We fear for our lives."

Michihara sighed. Slowly he rose, carefully picking straw from his kimono. "Noguchi, I do not wish to fight. Therefore, you *cannot* defeat me."

His calm voice made Noguchi furious. "You carry the swords of the samurai, old man. Have you no longer the might of the samurai?"

"I need neither swords nor might to defeat you. But let us not trouble these good people with our quarrel."

Michihara pointed across the water. "There, on one of the deserted islands near the shore, the greater samurai will prevail."

Noguchi pranced with excitement as they neared the island, so keen was he to prove once again that he was the best, the most ferocious samurai. He leapt from the bow and waded ashore with his sword held high above the sea.

Michihara removed his own long sword. Noguchi called,
"Do you still think you can defeat me without a sword, old man?"

"You raise your sword without understanding, Noguchi, so
even the boatman's bamboo pole can conquer you." Michihara
grabbed the pole and, with one great shove, he pushed the ship
back out to sea.

"Coward!" shouted Noguchi, as the ferry began to leave him behind. "Why do you not fight?"

"I *have* fought," Noguchi heard Michihara's voice call over the wind. "And, without a sword, I have defeated you. Wits are the best weapon of all."

With a fearsome cry, Noguchi threw off his kimono and
struggled through the churning waters.

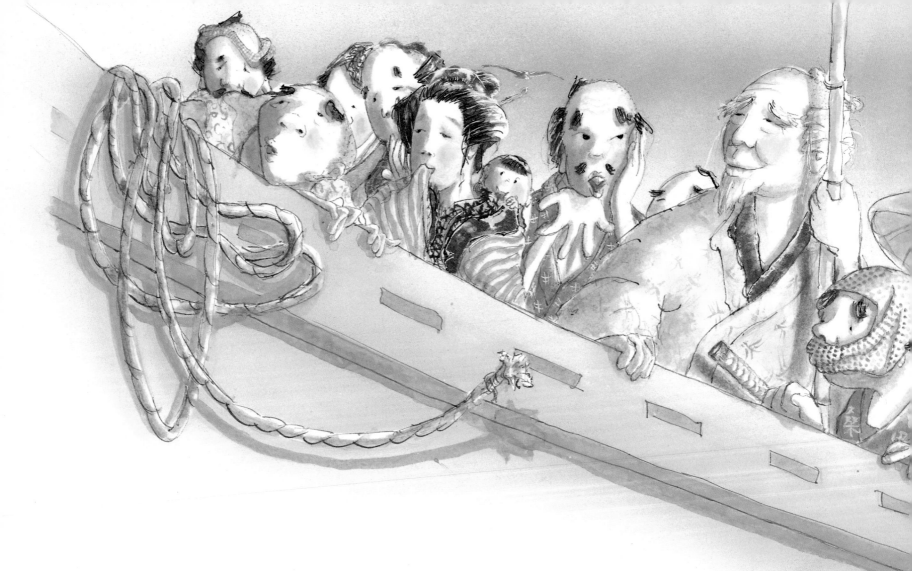

"Help, Michihara," cried Kuzu-ya, "he shall sink us all. Quick!
The boatman's pole!"

But Michihara calmly raised his hand. "No. Go back for him."

When Noguchi saw the ferry turn toward the island, he plucked his swords from the sand and retrieved his kimono. Cautiously, the passengers pulled Noguchi onto the deck, unsure of what the sodden samurai might do. Kuzu-ya gingerly offered Noguchi his pipe.

Noguchi donned his kimono and swords in silence. Clutching Kuzu-ya's pipe, he bowed deeply before Michihara. "Today you have taught me what it means to be a true samurai."

Michihara smiled beneath his straw hat.
He offered his tea cup to Noguchi. "In losing,
my friend, you have won something
deeper than the sea."